Valentine Mice!

Valentine Mice!

by Bethany Roberts
Illustrated by Doug Cushman

Clarion Books • New York

Clarion Books
a Houghton Mifflin Company imprint
215 Park Avenue South, New York, NY 10003
Text copyright © 1997 by Barbara Beverage
Illustrations copyright © 1997 Doug Cushman

The illustrations for this book were executed in watercolor.
The type was set in 21/24-point Cantoria semi bold.

Printed in the USA.

Library of Congress Cataloging-in-Publication Data

Roberts, Bethany.
Valentine mice! / by Bethany Roberts ; illustrated by Doug Cushman.
p.   cm.
Summary: An energetic group of mice deliver valentines to the other animals.
ISBN 0-395-77518-3   PA ISBN 0-618-05152-X
[1. Valentines—Fiction. 2. Mice—Fiction.] I. Cushman, Doug, ill. II. Title.
PZ7.R5396Val   1997
[E]—dc21   96-50889
                                                            CIP
                                                            AC

WOZ 10 9 8 7 6 5

To my valentines
Bob, Krista and Melissa
—*B. R.*

To Juney Irene Cushman, my first valentine
—*D. C.*

Valentine mice
deliver valentines—

red, pink.
Skip! Hop!

Up this hill,
then s-l-i-d-e down.

One little mouse
goes *swoosh*! Plop!

One to the rabbit,
two for the squirrels,

three for the chipmunks.
Zip! Nip!

More to deliver.
Cross the pond.

S-l-i-d-e!   G-l-i-d-e!

14

Slip!

Flip!

15

Valentines here!

Valentines there!

Shower valentines!

THROW! THROW! THROW!

Valentine mice—
one, two, three . . .

One is missing!
Where can he be?

Valentine mice
look high and low.

Hurry! Worry!
Call! Shout!

Follow these footprints.
Quick! Quick!

There's a mitten!

Pull him out!

All together now . . .

Dig!   Tug!

Push! P-u-l-l!

YAY!

One little mouse gets a

valentine hug.